Love The Only Language

An Anthology Shedding Light on Various Shades of Love

Writernaama Book Club

Printed in India.

Contents

Algira Pereira

Algira Pereira, a self-proclaimed favourite of her own story, thrives in the corporate wilderness by seeking contempt in the profound art of questioning, skilfully crafting insightful articles, and creating poetry that resonates with every emotion. Algira as a person believes in continuous learning and exploring new subjects, affirms that each of us holds the potential to create our own destiny, and with the right mindset and determination, we can transform our dreams into reality.

The Unspoken Legacy by Algira

The wedding venue, nestled on the outskirts of Seattle, USA, was a vision of ethereal beauty. Rows of chairs, lovingly adorned in hues of ivory and pastels, guests to settle in for the celebration. The pavilion at its heart, dressed in billowing fabrics and fragrant blossoms, stood as a symbol of love's grand stage. As the sun dipped below the horizon, lanterns along the pathway lit up like stars, creating a path awash in warm, romantic hues. A quartet of musician's harmonious tunes floated like whispers on the breeze. Children darted playfully around the venue, their laughter an infectious melody that echoed the happiness in every heart.

As the guests arrived, their steps slowed down as they entered the enchanting space. The sight that greeted them stole their breath away, and a collective gasp of awe rippled through the assembly.

As the sun descended, casting a warm, amber glow over the venue, in the dressing room Lisa stood as the epitome of radiant beauty. Her gown, a masterpiece of lace and satin, flowed like a river of dreams, and her veil trailed behind her like a whisper of anticipation. She was ready for her big day. Lisa's heart was aflutter, for she knew that any moment now, her father would appear at the door, ready to escort her down the aisle.

Meanwhile, outside the dressing room, the camera captured the flurry of activity among the guests who had arrived for the ceremony. Some stood in awe, still mesmerised by the venue's enchanting decor, while others nibbled on delectable snacks, savouring each bite as they soaked in the atmosphere. The quartet's music continued to serenade those who found solace in its harmonious notes, and praises for the meticulous decorations echoed throughout the venue. Glasses clinked as guests raised toasts, sharing in the joy of the impending union. Laughter and conversation filled the air like the lively backdrop of a heartfelt celebration.

As the appointed time for the nuptials to begin drew near, the priest at the altar cast furtive glances at his wrist, anxiety gnawing at him. Whispers rippled through the assembled guests, their voices growing hushed as uncertainty filled the air.

Lisa's bridesmaids exchanged concerned glances, their attempts to reassure her now tinged with their growing apprehension. Time was slipping away, and the anticipation outside was reaching fever pitch.

Suddenly, a hand descended gently on Lisa's shoulder, and she thought it was her father. But as she turned, she was met with the quizzical, worried gaze of Daniel, her fiancé.

"Where are Mom and Dad?" Daniel's voice trembled with concern as he asked the question that hung heavy in the room.

Lisa's eyes welled with tears as she blinked back at the panic threatening to engulf her. "I don't know," she whispered, her voice barely audible above the pounding of her heart. The realisation that her parents were missing at this crucial moment sent shockwaves of fear and confusion through her, threatening to unravel the meticulously planned day.

As Daniel moved to console Lisa, trying to find words of comfort during the turmoil, Vincent, Lisa's cousin, approached with a grave expression etched on his face. He carried with him the heavy news that Lisa's brother, Andrew, had suffered a brain stroke and that her parents were at the hospital by his side.

The words hit Lisa like a tidal wave, and she felt her world crumble. The joy and anticipation of her wedding day had collided head-on with the devastating news of her beloved brother's health. Her legs gave way, and she sank to the ground, overcome with grief and despair.

Sobs wracked her body as she grappled with the impossible choice that fate had thrust upon her. Her heart ached for her brother, and yet here she was, dressed in her bridal gown, her happiness shattered by the cruel hand of destiny. The clash of emotions was overwhelming, leaving her torn between the love for her family and the commitment she had made to Daniel.

Lisa's world had spiralled into a whirlwind of heartache, and the joyous occasion had taken an unexpected, painful turn.

As memories from her childhood flashed before her eyes, Lisa felt an overwhelming wave of emotion crashing down on her. In that moment of vulnerability, she couldn't help but reflect on her life and the moments when her parents were conspicuously absent. It wasn't just about this critical day but a pattern of absence that stretched back to her earliest memories.

She remembered her first day of school, the excitement in her heart, the shiny new backpack, and the feeling of stepping into the unknown. But her parents hadn't been there to share that moment. They had been absent during her school plays, too. She had spent weeks crafting costumes and rehearsing tirelessly, but their seats had remained empty in the audience.

Her graduation had been another milestone where their absence had cast a shadow over her achievement. Even when she had recently received the best photographer award, a recognition she had worked so hard for, her parents had not been there to witness her triumph.

A bitter truth began to crystallise in her mind: her parents had never been there when she needed them the most, and the excuse, as she saw it now, was always her brother Andrew. The clash between her family's demands and her dreams had left her feeling neglected and unfulfilled.

As these thoughts swirled through her mind, the weight of her emotions intensified, leaving her torn between her love for her family and the realisation that she had made sacrifices throughout her life. The clash of emotions, the desire to be with her brother in his time of need, and the promise she had made to Daniel had turned her world into a tumultuous sea of conflicting emotions.

Daniel was diagnosed with autism in his early birthdays. The attention required by Daniel was immense, to the point that when he grew, he couldn't be handled by one person alone. He had no cognitive abilities and no physical abilities. Both of her parents had been tirelessly occupied in caring for him for over a decade, ensuring that he received the care and support he needed.

Lisa was sobbing uncontrollably and almost reaching the level of anger and searching for answers to her questions; an elderly lady's voice cut through the air, commanding Lisa's attention, "In her childhood, Lisa had been Andrew's guardian angel. She had held him close, guiding him with love and patience through each step of life. Lisa had been his constant companion, taking him along wherever she ventured, treating him not as a burden but as her cherished friend. Their bond had been unbreakable. Lisa had played with Andrew, shared secrets with him, and bestowed upon him the unconditional love that only a sister could. She had never felt ashamed of her brother's disability, and her love for him had been as pure as the morning sun. Lisa had stood as a fortress, shielding Andrew from the cruelties of the world. Whenever other kids teased him, she had been his fierce protector. Her laughter had been his greatest joy, and she had always captured moments of his happiness on video, playing them back to him whenever he needed a reason to smile."

These words had provided solace and understanding to Lisa and had helped her uncover her unspoken and unexpressed love for her brother, Andrew.

With a gentle and loving touch, Daniel reached out and held Lisa's hand. Without uttering a single word, he communicated his support and understanding. Lisa, her eyes filled with gratitude for Daniel's understanding, nodded silently.

Daniel, taking charge of the situation, stepped forward to address the crowd that had gathered. His voice, steady and resolute, conveyed the difficult decision they had made. "Ladies and gentlemen," he began, "we have decided to postpone our wedding to a future date. Right now, our priority is to be with Lisa's brother, Andrew, who needs us."

Lisa now changed to simpler attire, felt a mixture of emotions as she prepared to leave for the hospital. She was grateful for the love and understanding of those around her, especially Daniel, who had stood by her side through it all. With Daniel and Vincent by her side, she rushed to the hospital, ready to be there for her brother, Andrew.

Lisa's heart ached as she entered the hospital room and found her parents sitting by Andrew's bedside, their faces etched with worry and lost hope. Seeing her mother's eyes, Lisa sensed the unspoken remorse and pain her mother carried. It was a moment of realisation for Lisa, understanding that her parents had always done their best, even if circumstances had often pulled them apart.

Her gaze then fell upon her beloved brother, Andrew, lying in the hospital bed. Tears welled up in her eyes as she approached him, a flood of emotions overwhelming her. She prayed silently for his recovery, every fibre of her being yearning for his well-being.

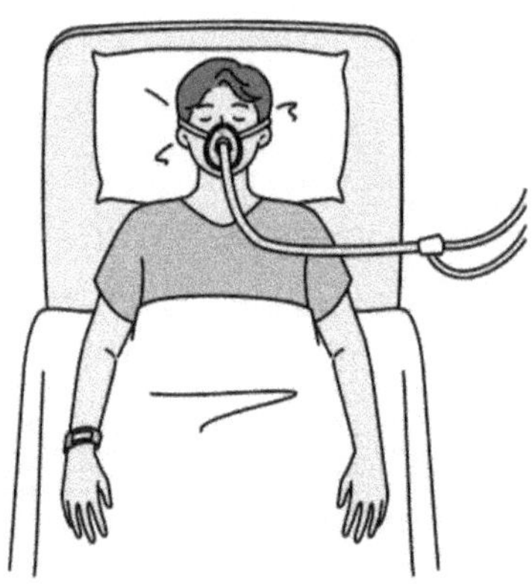

Lisa adjusted herself by Andrew's bedside, gently taking his hand in hers. She could feel the warmth of his hand, a connection that transcended words. All she wanted was for her brother to recover, to see him smile again, and to let him know how much she loved him.

As her tears fell onto Andrew's hand, she whispered, "Andrew, I need you now, and I love you." The words, though simple, carried the weight of a lifetime of love and devotion. Andrew had been an inspiration to many, and Lisa wanted him to know that his existence had enriched her life in immeasurable ways. She continued to hold his hand, her presence a silent vow to stand by him through this challenging time.

In that poignant moment, as Lisa held her brother's hand and professed her love, Andrew, with a faint smile, opened his eyes. His gaze met Lisa's, and a sense of peace seemed to wash over him. It was as though he had been waiting for this final connection with his sister as if Andrew knew it all but didn't know how to express it.

With that gentle smile still on his lips, Andrew took a slow, deep breath, and then, in the quiet of the hospital room, he exhaled for the last time. His journey had come to an end, leaving behind a legacy of love, inspiration, and the deep bond he shared with his family.

Lisa, her heart heavy with grief yet filled with the profound love they had shared, leaned in closer, tears streaming down her cheeks, and whispered, "Goodbye, Andrew." His smile, a testament to the love they had shared, remained etched in her memory as a bittersweet reminder of the profound impact he had on her life.

In that room, surrounded by the love of her family, Lisa said farewell to her beloved brother, whose spirit would forever live on in the cherished memories they had created together.

Lisa's heartache was immeasurable, having lost her dear brother Andrew. Yet, in the middle of this profound sorrow, she came to realise a powerful truth about love. It transcended definitions, categories, and expectations. It could manifest in countless forms, and her brother, despite his limitations, had been a profound source of love and inspiration throughout her life.

Andrew, unable to speak or perform many of the tasks most people took for granted, had demonstrated love through the unspoken language of his presence. His existence had reshaped their family's understanding of love, teaching them that it could be found in the everyday moments of care and devotion. It was a nurturing spring of emotional sustenance that had flowed quietly within their family, strengthening their bonds day by day.

On this day, Lisa found herself embracing this redefined love more deeply than ever before. It was a love that didn't require words, deeds, or expectations; it was simply about being there for one another.

Charmila M Sankar

After being a freelance writer for more than 10 years, Charmila M Sankar began to pursue her first love of writing fiction during lockdown. Her work has appeared in The Hindu – Young World, Kitaab, Woman's Era, Yuan Yang - A Journal of Hong Kong and International Writing, etc. She also published her collection of short stories titled, 'The Unwanted Boy and Other Stories' last year.

Serendipity by Charmila

I felt the wet grass sneak into the gaps of my sandals as I meandered towards the tree with a hole. The blades were sharp against my ankles, and the sensation made me shiver. It was silly of me to even think that she could be trapped inside. But I had to see it to believe it. No stone unturned, I thought as I walked around the tree. She wasn't there. As darkness descended, it made me envision creepy crawlies that could be lurking in the grass, waiting to reveal themselves.

I couldn't bear the idea that one of them might just crawl up my leg and maybe, just maybe, be poisonous. 'Okay, time to stop thinking,' I said to myself, trying to put my irrational fears to rest. But I couldn't help imagining what might have happened to Kimmy. How could I just abandon her in the middle of nowhere? I felt a sharp pang of guilt. What I did was not just unwise but horribly irresponsible.

Kimmy was more than a pet. For years, I had often asked my mom to get me a puppy, but she always refused. "Raising you is a task by itself. Don't bring a puppy into the mix," she'd always say. It was a fair argument, but I refused to accept defeat. I was so persistent and had to throw a few tantrums before she dragged me down to an animal shelter. The moment I saw Kimmy, I knew I had to have her.

She was inestimably cute. The best thing was how she worked her magic on my mom by reaching her hand out to her first. Though mom acted as if she was getting Kimmy only because of my demands, it was evident that she had instantly fallen in love with her. My heart aches at the reflection of what I did to someone who loved us unconditionally.

Even if I was really frustrated with her as she kept following me everywhere, I should not have tried to dodge her. I should have ridden back home and tied her to the pillar. Instead, I was crazy enough to drive through these narrow streets—stupid me. What I did weighed heavily on my conscience. How could I not even stop to pick her collar up when she dropped it? I presumed she would go back home. But she didn't. All because I was rushing to get the Pokémon card my classmate promised me. I couldn't care less about the card now.

Was she lost? Did someone take her? My nerves shuddered to even think about it. If I couldn't find Kimmy, I don't think I would be able to forgive myself, and I am sure Mom wouldn't forgive me either. Maybe I'll just run away from home too.

At that moment, in the far-off distance, I heard a bark. Faint but distinct. It was definitely a puppy. I stopped and listened keenly. The same sound that gave us sleepless nights the first week she came home. It could only be Kimmy. I began to run towards the sound.

The barking led me to a cosy cottage with a tiled roof. With dim lighting and fairy lights adorning the wooden porch, the house looked mystical. I hesitated as I climbed every step. I stood by the door, listening and waiting to see if anybody came by. But there was not much action except for the barking, which now came from inside the house.

I tried to look through the door opening, but nothing was visible because of the mesh door they had installed. With no other option, I rang the bell beside the name board that read -Advocate Sreemathi. Footsteps came closer and closer. A middle-aged woman of about fifty swung open the door, and tagging along was an enthusiastic dog.

"Kimmy!" I exclaimed, dropping to my knees. She dashed towards me and clutched my legs. Jumping frantically from side to side, she barked till my ears hurt. I couldn't decipher her language, but I could sense she was pretty mad at me. I said 'Sorry' and bent down to hug her, but she playfully toppled me over and pounced on me.

The woman walked up to us and said, "Jim, let our guest go." She then turned towards the house and yelled, "Pavan, come and tie the dog or take him in the back, will you?"

I gathered my courage and said, "Ma'am, I think this is my dog, Kimmy. I lost her this afternoon.

"What? Oh, I feel sorry for you, dear, but you are mistaken. That's our Jim. He does get very friendly with everyone. He wants to make many friends. Jumps on everybody but a harmless little puppy," she said with hands on her hips.

While I was pondering on how to convince her, a young boy about my age rolled in on a wheelchair. Kimmy immediately rushed to him and tried to jump on him, too. The boy laughed and batted the puppy's paws, indicating him to settle down. Kimmy turned towards me and yelped. She was trying to tell me something, but I was blank.

The woman softly said, "It has been years since Pavan has laughed like that." It was more to herself than to me.

Suddenly, it dawned on me that this boy needed Kimmy more than me. He needed the kind of love only Kimmy was capable of. The love she gave Mom and me. The love that is so pure and unconditional. I knew what I had to do.

"Maybe I was mistaken. I should get going. It's late already." I said, my voice trembling. Taking a step back, I began to walk away.

Just as I reached the last step, the woman called out to me. "I am sorry, dear. I truly am. I don't know what came over me. Seeing Pavan so happy after a long time made me lose my mind." She hesitated for a moment and then continued gently grazing Pavan's head. "We found this dog on our doorstep. He was scratching at the door. He was so adorable that I had to let him in. If you are sure that he's your dog, he probably is. Please take him along with you. You seem to be a lovely boy. You do not deserve to lose your dog like this."

No matter how much they insisted, I refused to take Kimmy with me. But when Pavan said, "I will never be free of guilt if you don't take him with you... Please," my heart dropped. Reluctantly, I agreed.

"But I have a request. Hope you won't say no to it," I asked.

"Yes," both of them said in unison and listened intently.

"I wish I could come here once in a while with Kimmy and play with Pavan if that's okay with you. I'm new to town and don't have many friends."

They smiled and nodded while the woman patted me on my shoulders. "Sure, you and this little guy are welcome anytime. She tickled Kimmy under her chin the way she liked.

"It's girl, by the way. Kimmy is a girl," I added, and we all laughed. I left their house contented that I had found Kimmy and gained a friend in the process.

Nirupama Guha

Nirupama Guha, author of Soulful Snapshots, combines 14 years of corporate experience, marriage, motherhood, and 3 years of coaching, becoming known for her empathy. She gracefully maintains a balance between her personal life, professional life, memory coaching radiating perpetual growth and a warm smile.

Love's Ripple Effect by Nirupama

On a bustling Saturday afternoon, I found myself immersed in household chores. It was 11:30 AM, and I suddenly realized that it was high time to start preparing lunch, considering I had already procrastinated. My husband was returning from a week-long official trip to Mumbai, and he was bringing along a senior officer we had invited for lunch. I had decided on the food menu, but it needed careful planning and execution. I wanted to include chicken curry, the popular Bengali Prawn Malai curry, a Paneer Dish, Dal, Rice, Kheer, and a few other accompaniments - all cooked at home with love and respect for our much-awaited guest.

I'm the type of person who has trouble saying no when someone needs help, especially if I can do something about it. Just as I was getting ready to cook, my friend called. We'd been talking about his career change for a few days, and this Saturday was an important day for him.

Friend: (Anxious) "Hey, I really need your advice on this. It's a make-or- break moment for me today."

Me: (Politely) "I understand, but I'm a bit occupied right now. Can I 0067et back to you later this afternoon?"

Friend: (Relieved) "Sure, I appreciate that. Take your time, however, I will leave a few text messages. Please check and respond; it's a bit urgent."

Me: (Assuring) "Sure, I can do that."

My phone rang, and it was a video call from my husband.

Husband: "Security check-in is done. We are seated near the boarding gate, taking off in another 30 minutes."

Before I could check if the menu was okay with him, he slid the phone toward the senior police officer who was our guest for the day. We exchanged greetings and pleasantries, and I concluded by saying, "Looking forward to meeting you, Sir," with a broad smile. I then dropped a message to my husband, requesting him to please call me as soon as he lands or while taxiing.

As I began gathering cooking ingredients, I realized I was out of Paneer & Ghee, a key component of two of the dishes. Typically, I would delegate such tasks to my husband when he did our weekly grocery shopping, but he was away. I had no choice but to order online, something I wasn't fond of.

Amidst juggling between cooking tasks and responding to my friend's urgent messages, I quickly placed an order online. The clock was ticking, and I was racing against time.

Me: (Frustrated) "I hope this delivery comes on time. I really need these key ingredients in a flash."

I soon realized that I hadn't set a reminder for the delivery time since online grocery shopping wasn't something I usually did. Panicking, I checked the order status on my laptop. To my dismay, it said the order had been delivered at 12:30 PM. I rushed to the door, but there were no bags in sight. I felt a tightening in my throat, anxiety creeping in, my fingers went numb.

Me: (Anxious) "What do I do now? Should I call customer care? Should I ask my husband to follow up on this when he lands?"

My kids had never handled an online inquiry like this before, and I was hesitant about asking them to call customer care. If I made them call, I'd have to guide them through the process of choosing options on the IVR and providing the necessary information.

Just as my frustration reached its peak, I received a call from an unknown number. It was the delivery person.

Delivery Person: (Polite) "Madam, I have arrived at your location."

Me: Rushed to the doorstep, I looked down towards the road and found him on a bike with a helmet on and a bag in his hand. "Why did you mark the order as delivered before you even got here? Ok please come now and handover the items."

Delivery Person: (Calm) As he reached my doorstep at the first floor, "I'm sorry, madam. There was a railway gate closure that delayed me, so I closed the order to avoid further issues on my delivery timelines. But I have all your items."

As he took off his helmet, I looked at his face, I noticed he was bit senior in age, the few grey hair, and the wrinkles.

Me: (Guilty) "I'm sorry for being harsh earlier. Thank you for bringing the groceries."

Back in the kitchen, I couldn't shake off the guilt I felt for my initial reaction.

Me: (Reflecting) “I need to remember to treat people with kindness and respect, regardless of their age and profession.”

This incident prompted me to gather my kids and share the story with them.

Me: (Thoughtful) "What do you think we should do in such situations, kids?"

Before my kids could answer, my friend called again.

Friend: (Urgent) "I really need your help. Can you please give me some guidance?"

Me: (Compassionate) "I promise I'll get back to you within the next couple of hours. Hang in there."

And getting back to my kids, I was reassured that Kids often have a unique perspective, and I was eager to hear theirs. They responded with empathy and understanding.

With a newfound sense of compassion and understanding, I returned to the kitchen to complete my cooking.

Me: (Reassuring) "We should always try to be kind and considerate, no matter what."

As I resumed my chores, my phone rang again. It was my husband calling.

Me: (Answering with concern) "Have you arrived?"

Husband: "Not yet, the flight is delayed by 45 minutes. Just wanted to keep you informed."

To my surprise, I felt a rush of happiness at the news of his delayed flight. It was a blessing in disguise.

Me (to myself): "That's great! I have some extra time now to get everything ready and to reflect on how love and compassion can make a big difference in our interactions with others."

After closing the pressure cooker, I took a moment to relax on my recliner. I also picked up my phone to respond to my friend's unread messages.

Our guest arrived with a cheerful demeanour and spent quality time engaging my twin kids with his wealth of knowledge and educational guidance. They had lively discussions about football, competitive exams, and the importance of discipline and7 early preparation for higher education. Although I had met Sir three years ago when he hosted us at his home in Mangalore, my husband had uttered some random menu caused butterflies in my stomach as I wasn't entirely aware of his food preferences. I was delighted to see him relish everything I served on his plate. He blessed us before leaving in the evening.

Later that night, my friend called with exciting news – he had successfully negotiated a deal with his employer. I could hear the joy in his voice, and it warmed my heart.

And there it was, the ripple effect of love and compassion that had started with a simple act of understanding and kindness had now extended to the field executives, our guest, the food we prepare daily, my friend, and my family. It made me realize that in a world where we often rush through our daily lives, a little empathy and patience can create a ripple effect of positivity, touching the lives of everyone we meet.

Pradeep Tandon

Hailing from Lucknow, Pradeep Tandon is a former banker. He is the author of his debut novel 'The Real Thakur.' The second book,' The Curse of a Comet' is in the pipeline. His literary portfolio extends beyond novels, with a collection of soul-stirring poems and engaging short stories. Yet, at the core of his creative aspirations lies the dream of becoming a screenwriter, breathing life into stories that transcend the pages of a book.

Whispers to the Moon by Pradeep

The story unfolds in a quaint, picturesque, remote village of Manipur, within the arms of a rolling hill, where diverse communities reside together. Out of their religious beliefs, two dominant communities were more often than not at daggers drawn. As this village was cut off from the mainstream, the villagers were consumed by superstition, misconceptions, and ignorance. The village also lacked medical facilities and education.

James was a vibrant, warm-hearted, and handsome youth with a heart full of dreams of making big in the world. His biggest dream was to bring warring communities closer together.

Sarah was a young girl of unwavering determination, beautiful, wise, and much ahead of her time.

One day, she found her father, Rameshwar Narain, in a jolly state of mind.

She said, "Papa, I want to go to school to learn more about life."

"You know Sarah, I have given you enough education at home. You can read and write well. Is that not enough? Now, we have begun searching for a good match for you."

"Sorry, papa, but just being literate is like just tasting one bite from the whole apple of knowledge and wisdom. In fact, why only me? I want to have that apple for all in Manipur. I want to re-paint the canvas of their mind to dispel ignorance, disbelief, and superstition. And paint it with the colours of knowledge, wisdom, harmony, and prosperity.

Rameshwar Narain was dumbfounded. He needed no more words when he could see a reflection of what was coming next once he had educated her. He tried the last ace up his sleeves to dissuade her.

"Oh! Sarah, tell me. Aren't we adhering to our traditions? Have we not become more peaceful and prosperous? Isn't school a common place where youngsters from different communities mingle and develop emotions, particularly girls? Aren't results often disastrous?"

"Have faith in your daughter, papa. I wouldn't do anything that goes against tenets laid down by our ancestors." Sarah insisted while pleading with a puppy face.

"OK, Sarah, I grant you your wish, but always remember, between daughter and family's honour, it will always be the latter I would uphold."

James was in the same school; he and Sarah had the same aspirations. While fighting for the same cause, they fell head over heels for each other. When it fell on Rameshwar Narain's ears, he burnt in anger and immediately pulled Sarah out of school. Sarah was now under the radar for nuptial preparations. The situation turned tinder box between the two communities.

Love is not just blind but also deaf. When Rameshwar Narain tried to restrain his daughter from meeting James, she began to meet him in the precinct of the church. Henry, another youth of courage, determination, and a very close and loyal friend of James, kept vigil at the church's entrance to forewarn the love birds, of any eventuality.

For many days, James didn't venture out of his house to meet Sarah.

As Sarah and Henry lived close by. Sarah asked Henry, "I haven't seen James for many days. Is there any problem with him.?

"I met him a week back; he had a temperature and severe cold and acute congestion. I didn't hear anything from him since then, as I was also preoccupied with my father's illness." Replied Henry.

"Henry, let's go and find out?" Said Sarah, looking worried.

When they reached James, they were shocked to find him feeble, suffering from an acute cold, lung infection and fever.

Sarah knew one Vaidya ji who belonged to her community. He gave James some medicines, but those didn't help the cause.

Meanwhile, as the news of his condition spread out of fear and ignorance, the villagers chose to isolate him. But when some deaths were reported where he lived, the pitch for his banishment turned into a crescendo.

Sarah wanted to take the help of her father, but she knew that the sheer mention of James would be like knowingly burning oneself in his fiery rage. What she did not know was that the rumour of corona was knowingly spread like wildfire as revenge by her father.

Sarah, a woman of unwavering determination, refused to distance herself from James. Disease didn't dampen her fire of love. She and Henry defied the villagers' glances and embarked on a journey of perseverance to support hapless James, who required support and love to overcome the illness that was not coronavirus.

But in the end, the efforts of Sarah and Henry were dwarfed by the guiles of Rameshwar Narain. Protesters were manipulated, and James was banished to a very high mountain's tabletop far away from the village. The place was shrouded with mystery and seemed to be whispering close to the stars and the moon.

Isolated, James managed to build a tree house, and fruit availability was enough to take care of his survival needs. As the night fell, the Moon and stars came very close, as if they wanted to whisper something to him. He moved closer to the edge of the tabletop to have a clearer view of them and sat under a tree. He watched them closely for a long time. Soon, he was lost in an overwhelming feeling of love for Sarah. Down below, far away, he could see the glow of the flickering lights of his village.

At the mountaintop, every night, James would whisper his thoughts to the moon as if it were a silent messenger to Sarah, his beacon of hope. Soon, he realised that when he sat on a small stump-- under the tree-- on the edge of the mountain, he saw a glimpse of his beloved's reflection in the moon.

Sarah always felt that James would be desperately looking for her from the hilltop. She could hear the whispers of the moon calling her. As the night descended, a cascade of emotions surged within her. Listening to the echoes of her heartbeats, she would silently tread towards her terrace to listen to the moon's call and came on the terrace every night to hear and see her beloved's reflection in the moon. Their love was a force that had transcended the barriers of reality, moved the moon to become amiable, and ignited a flame that neither distance nor illness could vanquish.

Sarah came religiously every night to talk to her beloved; their love blossomed and grew more intense. Her unwavering devotion became a lifeline for James, infusing him with strength to battle isolation and illness. Their heartfelt feelings were carried by the wind and penned on the face of the Moon; they shared their dreams, fears, and unwavering commitment to each other. James began to convalesce and gain in strength.

Then, one day, the weather played a spoilsport. It rained and rained ceaselessly, and after that, fog and mist remained for months together. Weather played truant at the mountaintop only, whereas it remained normal at Sarah's. Rain and mist at James' place obscured the moon's tender glow, severing the ethereal connection between them. Their messages remained unsent and unheard.

In the absence of their moonlit conversation, despair began to take hold of Sarah's heart. Convinced that James was lost to her forever, she reluctantly agreed to the marriage, though her soul could not embrace the very idea.

When the weather relented and the sky cleared, the moon and stars reappeared; the connection was restored. James met with a heart-wrenching truth that shattered his dreams. Reflection on the moon of Sarah, adorned in bridal finery, her hand interwind with another's. The realisation that time had slipped through his fingers like grains of sand left him speechless, his heart aching with pain he had never known.

It was a case of do or die for James; he knew that he had lost his Sarah and a part of him was dead. With Sarah lost to him, he knew a painful death was imminent. He tried desperately to connect with Sarah through the wind and the moon, but in vain. As certain of James' death, she had long considered it futile to walk to the terrace and whisper her intense love. So, despite James' summons, Sarah's heart turned deaf.

Putting his life in peril, he descended the mountain and headed for Sarah's home to apprise her of his existence.

When he reached the venue, Sarah was about to garland the bride-groom when their eyes met. She became hysterical; leaving the garland behind, she ran and embraced James. Both of them broke down, oblivious to the fact that the bridegroom's side and her father were smarting under the humiliation.

Bride-groom snapped his garland, their side accused Rameshwar Narain for keeping them in the dark and threatened to return without marriage. In a fit of anger,

Rameshwar Narain fired at the James. Sarah flung herself in front of James, taking the bullet intended for James.

Cradling her in his arms, James cried in deep anguish, “What have you done, Sarah? Do you think I can live without you?”

“James, where were you? You made me wait for too long.”

“Sarah, I have come forever. Nobody can separate us now.”

“Yes, forever, my love,” Sarah said with a weak smile, and she passed out.

In the meantime, violence broke out between the two communities. Henry helped James escape by grievously hurting Sarah in a car at the base of the hilltop. Reunion with Sarah gave strength to James to carry the injured Sarah with him on the rope ladder. James was about to reach the mountaintop when Rameshwar Narain reached the spot and fired at him. The bullet pierced James’ thigh; he dangled precariously on the rope. When he was about to fire again, Henry and his men killed him. James managed to reach the tabletop.

The village that once buzzed with activities wore a haunted look now.

Sarah's condition worsened, her life hanging by a fragile thread. Weak and fading, she managed to communicate with James through the moon one last time. Her whispered words carried across the void, a declaration of love and a plea for him to remember her. And then, as the moon's light shone its brightest, Sarah breathed her last, leaving her spirit becoming one with the celestial realm.

With Sarah's passing, James was crestfallen. The tabletop mountain that had once been a sanctuary of hope now seemed a desolate wasteland of sorrow. The pain of his loss was a suffocating weight, dragging him deeper into the abyss of his illness. He no longer had anything to hold on to, and the desire to continue fighting dwindled with each passing day. As the seasons changed once more, James' frail form became a mere echo of the vibrant man he had once been. His body weakened, his spirit broken, and he found himself yearning for the release of death's embrace. He would gaze at the moon, now a haunting reminder of the love that had been lost, and pray for its light to guide him into eternity. And so, within the embrace of the moonlight that had witnessed their love's journey, James surrendered to the inevitability of his fate. The village that had banished him, the love that had sustained him, and the moon that had connected their souls – all were now distant memories, etched into the annals of a tragic and bittersweet love story that defied the boundaries of life and death.

To know the fate of his friend, Henry ventured to the mountain top, only to find James dead. Lamenting his friend's loss, he buried James beside Sarah's grave. The night fell; it was a full moon night. The moon and stars came very close and shone brightly; the whole area bathed under the celestial lights. Lamenting, he coincidentally ventured to the edge, sat on the stump under the tree and looked at the moon. I was amazed to see the reflection of James and Sarah communicating in whispers and poetic lines scribbled below it. Perhaps it was the message the moon wanted to convey to the world through him.

Whisper of love on the moonlit breeze;

Hearts entwined with tender ease.

But storms of sorrow swept away;

Love's connection, come what may.

Rain-soaked skies, message lost;

Love's bridge was severed at a heavy cost.

Love The Only Language

A bullet's path, a loved one laid bare,

In the moon's glowing care, yet found despair.

Despair and death path one should shun;

For violence, it serves a purpose none.

Henry had the poem engraved on their tomb.

Legend has it that even today if any visitor happens to sit on the same stump under the tree and watch the moon, he witnesses the reflection of James and Sarah. Now, they share an unshakeable bond of eternal togetherness, and the moon is still a carrier of their silent whispers.

Sheenu Mehta

Sheenu Mehta considers myself a multi-faceted individual, adept at fulfilling various roles. Embracing the responsibilities of being a mother and a wife has ingrained within her an inherent sense of empathy, organization, and perseverance. As a tarot reader, she harnesses her intuitive abilities to offer seekers invaluable guidance and clarity. Her love for writing allows her to delve into her introspective nature, enabling her to share her distinctive perspective and forge deeper connections with others. Through her words, she aims to provide solace, empathy, or even a moment of reflection.

The Curious Case of Man with a Briefcase by Sheenu

Holding his briefcase tight to his chest, an elderly man walks out of a bank hurriedly; he then takes the last seat at the city bus stop and looks at his watch, "10 minutes to go", a voice breaks into his ears; he sees a young lad join next to him and gets seated staring at him from top to toe. "You seem to have got a lot of money with you. Shall I drop you home?"

Looking suspiciously at the young lad, "I can take care of myself, young man. Thanks for your concern."

"Of course, you can; maybe you need little company as the bus you wanted to board is cramped already. They both look at the bus as it passes by without stopping."

"I know a little coffee shop nearby. Probably we can go and have some together." The elderly man nodded.

The coffee's aroma is making the elderly man relax a bit. He loosens his grip on the bag and keeps it aside.

The young lad said, “A coffee can make you trust me with your bag!”

“it’s not about the bag anymore. It’s about you!

“Me?”

“Yes, you!”

“What’s with me?”

“How do you stay so un-loving?”

“What, wait, how can you even say that? We have just met, and you call me unloving, what makes you say that?”

“You being alone at this age, spying on an old man over coffee, is a sign that you have no other job in the world to do!”

“I thought you needed my help!”

“How many people do you help daily? Are you always available?”

“You are misunderstanding me, old man! Anyone can discover you have a treasure in your bag; any thief can easily snatch it and run away, and you won’t be able to utter a word, so I simply tried to protect you!”

"Yes, there is a treasure in my bag, but do not show mercy on me by protecting me when I didn't ask for it!"

"You are a thankless man; I shall keep going. You better stay alone here!"

"I don't mind being alone. I have always been like this!"

"You might be lucky to be able to enjoy loneliness, probably your forefathers were greatly rich!"

"What makes you so bitter? Money??"

"You say I sound bitter, what do you know about me, I never knew who my father was, my mother left me because her boyfriend didn't want me. I grew up yearning for love in a shelter home, watching other happy kids with their families around. I wanted to be a football player but always got kicked by others while I just wanted to play with them."

His face turned red, and his eyes were teary as he continued, "You know what, this world is merciless, unloving, and you all don't need care, just punishment for being so self-seeking." He picked up his bag and ran away as fast as he could.

The elderly man remains seated, relaxed with a grin for a while, then he gets up and leaves a note at the counter with the Barista and catches the next bus.

Sitting on a bench in an empty football stadium, the young man tried to open the bag, but to his surprise, there was no lock. He simply opened it and finds a book and a handwritten note.

The heading on the book cover read, "A day that stole thief's life."

He opens the handwritten note, which said "A learned person held my hand once as a child, when I was about to pick someone else's pocket. He asked me how much money I needed so that I didn't have to steal again. I kept counting on my little fingers but could not say one amount that would be sufficient for my whole life."

"The man then took me to his home and said, "Kid, there is no amount of money that can keep you contented all your life; however, instead, let me allow you to transform into someone who can live a contented life himself and also help people to choose to live life over surviving somehow."

P.S. You are reading my life story that soon will be yours too!!

At the back of the note, there was one address mentioned. It was the same café he took the elderly man to, it was written "Please return briefcase here, only after you read this book."

He read the book the whole night, and the next morning, when he reached to the counter at the café, the Barista looked at him and said, "You can place the briefcase on the shelf there (pointing to a drawer below the stairs)."

" How do you know I'm here to return the briefcase?"

Barista: "I saw you with that elderly man. He visits us regularly with some or the other new young man or woman, and the next day, they would come to return his stuff."

The young lad was shocked and taken aback, all this while the old man wanted him to run away with his briefcase! This is why he was rude towards him?? He was piled up with questions.

The barista hands him a note - "hey, this is for you."

It read, "I am glad you came. Meet me at the given address tomorrow morning at 10 am."

The young lad never waited for the new day so anxiously, just like he did that night!

As soon as he reaches the given location, he enquires about the magical man, the receptionist.

She takes him to a big hall, where there are about 50 people almost of his age.

The elderly man comes to the stage with a mic in his hand (to the young lad, he actually looks like a magician with a wand). He greeted each and every one present there, "I welcome my Phoenixes to the Odyssey with the new awareness you have gotten into.

Life happens every moment. We are reborn every moment and NOW is that moment. I wish you all a very happy Re-birthday! The days we lived till yesterday were our field experience. Now, with all that experience, we begin another project in our lives to become better versions of ourselves to change this world into a beautiful place.

From today, I will coach you to become life coaches!

Why only you, as some of you must be thinking?

If I teach those who have resources to learn, it will help them coach more like them, but when I teach you all, from different walks of life, who never had assistance available to them, you will feel more responsible towards people like you, who are lost in the huddle of life and will help them shape their lives.

The world will not change by empowering those who are already empowered. However, it will change only when I go to the places and bring those people who are abandoned by society and are misled with anguish.

With this hope, I go to that bank daily to withdraw treasures like you. Please join me in creating lives that matter. I want you all to know love is not what we get from relations, but love is what makes us good humans. When you recognize the pain of not finding love, you value the need to create love around you!

You too can be that next treasure.

Salt Water Heals Everything by Sheenu

The sky was a brilliant array of yellow, orange, and red, as the sun prepared to bid farewell to the night after a long day. The sounds of waves and music from distant cafes filled the air, creating a tranquil and meditative atmosphere. Walking hand in hand along the beach, Dev and Esha came upon a deep red tent with a luminous light emanating from its interior. Dev and Esha glanced at each other as their eyes sparkled, they took a few selfies with the tent before they curiously entered inside, where they found a circular table adorned with a violet altar cloth and a collection of burning sage was placed in a bowl. The aroma of sage was captivating and invigorating.

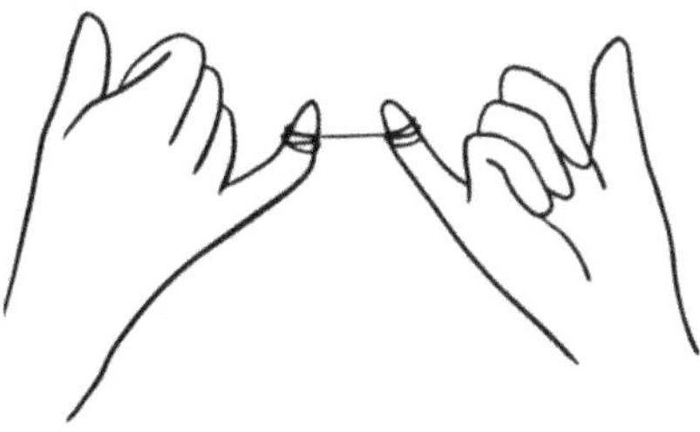

Ekaa suddenly showed up with a black pouch in her hand and said" it's no coincidence that you're here. "Archangel Michael sent me to guide both of you. Ask me."

Dev excitedly asked "when we will get married"?

She looked into their eyes and pulled out her tarot deck, shuffled it, and flipped three cards over.

They both looked at the cards and said, "What now?" She turns the card over and revealed" it's only going to get worse before it gets better. Stay strong and keep going!"

Dev looked disappointed and said, "You're trying to instil a fear in us for money to help! I don't believe in you; you only want us to keep coming to you."

Ekaa: "You think I care about money; I just warned you that it's your wish ahead! "

Dev walked out signalling Esha to follow, leaving money on the table.

Ekaa said, "You won't be able to hide this for long, either you'll own it or it'll come out and returned the money to Esha "I don't need money to guide souls He sends to me, I only wish you follow the right path." Esha looked tense and left without saying anything.

While walking towards the hotel Dev apologized to Esha, "I'm so sorry I took you there. Everything was going so great on our vacation. Let's grab a drink, okay? "

Esha agreed, smiling, and trying to forget what had just happened.

They sat close together in the bar, and Esha put her hand on Dev's shoulder. "You still think about that lady, don't you?" Dev enquired.

She nodded and said, "Can I ask you, if you're worried about us getting married someday?"

Dev smiled and took her hand in his, "We're already happy together, so what difference would it make if we got married? Do you see anything different in our love? Yeah, if you've already picked out a ring, I can give it to you right now." He winked.

She hugged him passionately, "I love you", both were lost once again in each other's company.

***

It's 9 am and Esha was ready for the office while Dev cuddled her from behind. She kissed Dev as he decided to go back to bed.

He's a cartoonist and pleasurably worked at his own pace. They both met for a project for Esha's magazine and fell in love over coffee dates and had been living together for five years. Both their families wanted them to get married sooner and were just waiting for the grand event they had dreamed of for them.

Esha was excited to get back to the office, she missed something terribly on vacation.

“Here you’re!!!” Preet called out from behind, "Oh my God, you almost killed me!" Esha put her hand to the chest and held her breath.

"C’mon I thought you were stronger than this! I am sure you had fun with Dev on vacation! It must have been refreshing to relax together after such a long time. So now, you'll be more focused at work and won't get lost anymore.”

Having said this, Preet looked inquiringly into Esha's eyes.

Esha took a moment to compose herself, then smiled and said, "Yeah, I'm quite charged up, everything will fall into place hopefully."

Esha was a passionate workaholic who worked as the creative head of a popular magazine and Preet joined her for six months. They had been inseparable since day one, and would never miss a day to hang out. People called them "Jay Veeru ki Jodi". Dev often joked to Preet about stealing his love, though Esha never seemed to really enjoy the joke, after the fateful day that started to make her feel lost.

It was during a fun activity, when Preet and Esha’s hands were tied together, Esha felt a sudden surge of emotion in her. She looked at Preet in confusion, when Preet pointed out towards the game, Esha could only nod at her, feeling worried about what she had just felt for her.

Since that day, she had been distracted at work and felt so differently towards Preet, like the way she felt towards Dev when they had met. This has caused her to feel guilty and perplexed at the idea of getting married to Dev, as it seemed like the most challenging task in the world to her.

Preet would often seek advice from Esha, bring her home-cooked meals and always be there for her. She was more than a mentor to her besides she was also friends with Dev. All she wanted was for them to be happy and dance until the last song is played on their wedding day.

Esha was trying to focus on her work while sipping her coffee and finalizing her cover page designs, when Preet suddenly appeared and offered to join her at a water fest that was taking place during the weekend. Esha was hesitant due to her fear of water, but Preet insisted her to join the underwater sports fest, saying that it is her birthday and she wanted to have fun with her favourite people. Esha was overwhelmed by her intense feelings for Preet, who took her hand and hugged her tightly. She couldn't say no and agreed to accompany her with Dev.

Esha was thinking all the time about the tarot reader's guidance, so she decided to call her but how? Suddenly she remembered the selfies they took outside and checked her phone and there she got her number written outside that deep red tent.

She decided to text Ekaa.

"Can you tell me why I am feeling so restless, what's going to happen? Esha"

Ekaa read the message and went into deep thought before she pulled two cards, "Three of swords" and "Tower" - it made her a little worried.

Esha's phone blinked.

Text from Ekaa: "Esha, own your truth before it's too late."

Esha gulped down her fear of not knowing what to do after she read the message.

Ekaa closed her eyes and sent healing energies to her.

***

Esha and Dev were all excited to join Preet on the beach that day.

Esha was having a good time with a drink and getting sunbathed, while Dev and Preet got ready to dive into the mysterious sea. After an hour of waiting, a boat arrived, but only the coach was there, and Dev and Preet couldn't be seen.

As soon as the boat reached the shore, the coach called emergency services to come and find them.

Esha enquired about what had happened to the coach, he informed that there was a huge rush of water causing both of them to disappear.

She broke and knelt at the shore, placed her hands in front of her face, praying and crying. After half an hour, a boat arrived with Preet at the shore. She was given first aid, as She opened her eyes, Esha rushed to her, thanking God that she was all right.

Esha asked her what had happened, where Dev was, why they had not found him with her, and if he was all right? She was in agony as she asked the questions.

Preet looked afraid and worried, tears rolled down her cheeks.

After a while, the two of them sat side by side, looking out to the sea, hoping to see Dev return with the search team.

Esha was reflecting on the moments she had spent with Dev teary-eyed as she remembered how much she missed him.

She was perplexed as to how she could be in love with both of them at once, which seemed unnatural to her. She was in a state of turmoil, her emotions caused her to break down at times. It was hard for her to admit this to anyone. However, her relationship with Dev was more mature than her love for Preet, which she had now come to terms with.

Then the sound of a helicopter approaching towards the shore brought her joy, she jumped to her feet as soon as she saw Dev getting out. She embraced him and began to hit him relentlessly.

She exclaimed and pleaded on her knees, "I'm so glad you're back, please marry me!!

"Woah don't kill me! I want to grow old with you! if I had known the proposal was coming, I would have jumped into the sea a long ago." Dev winked and pulled her up.

The two of them burst into laughter and embraced once again and looked madly in love.

Preet threw her arms around both of them, "I am so sorry that you had to go through all this, I would have never forgiven myself if something had happened to you."

"I must thank you for this journey Preet, it got me the marriage proposal I've been waiting for all my life, " Dev said happily.

"I am so happy for you two, let's get ready for D-Day, all three then hugged each other.

"Now I can share you with my wife."

This time Esha smiled without getting disturbed by Dev's joke anymore,

Preet got teary-eyed, "Thanks, but I'm not the home breaker, I just want you to be happy, you are both so special to me."

Esha held Dev's hands as they started to walk away, Preet stayed behind, "I'll join you in 5 minutes, got to freshen up".

"We are waiting for you Birthday Girl, Dress up your Best!!" Both chuckled.

She ran towards the restroom and burst aloud. She was both smiling and crying, muttering to herself, "I'm so sorry, God, I didn't mean to do this. I wanted to find out what was in Esha's heart, my joke went wrong today and we both must have ended up dead leaving Esha broken for life and I could have separated the true lovers."

She had always been fond of Esha, but never reciprocated her affection towards her, leaving Esha in a state of confusion.

Preet had difficulty having relationship with men. After meeting Esha, she realized her true feelings for her and decided to reveal only when she knew who She loved more, her or Dev.

Preet pulled her ears in apology as she silently thanked God for saving them from this misdeed. She wasn't sad that her love would never be fulfilled, however she was happy that Esha was no longer in a state of separation and could finally admit her true feelings for Dev!

***

Esha and Dev celebrated Preet's birthday together happily, despite a minor mishap.

Esha felt like texting Ekaa about what happened and ensuring the worst had gotten over.

“What do you see now?”

On Reading her text, Ekaa looked for answers by shuffling the cards.

Esha checked her cell phone as it buzzed a new notification.

Message from Ekaa.

“Ten of Cups: Time to start a journey towards being a happy family. Get Married and Have kids!”

Ekaa also got one card “Strength” that fell off on its own and she could sense there was someone who needed strength to bear the pain and come out as a stronger person than ever.

Ekaa closed her eyes and sent all of them a message of love and light. She felt a closure.

Preet had decided to stay alone and close to Esha and Dev as their best girl forever. She found her new strength in “being there” for them. True love is not about winning it's about caring for who you love, she learned this today.

The immense sea had solved the biggest mystery of their lives forever. Finally, Salt water has healed everything.

Suraj Shankar

Born in God's own country- Kerala, India, Suraj has contributed 25 years of his life to the country. Suraj being a conversationalist has been receptive, curious and has always been in an open frame. Suraj has painted a beautiful canvas of conversations with various people adding conversational colours in different strokes of life.

A Tale of the Rainy Season by Suraj

Hi, I am the Floor camera on the sixth floor of a decent society in the city called "Queen of the Arabian Sea' located in God's Own Country/State. It has people of various colours in a 256-shaded colour box.

We are many brothers and sisters, always connected and talking with one another. We understand each other very well and quickly inform each other of what happens anywhere in the area. Our core is located inside the building, the server room, which is the storehouse of all the things we see and convert into memories to store.

Unlike human friends, our memories are permanent and allow access anytime if the right combination of codes is pressed. So, what I am going to narrate is what any one of us would have observed. Our constant touch with one another allows all the parts we see to be woven into incredible stories of wonder. The stories are small and big, exciting and boring, right or wrong, perceived or reality, moody or ecstatic, joyous or sad, bright or dark, loud or silent, smooth or rough, black or white or coloured.

While many kinds of people live in our society, all of them fit with each other like the pieces of a jigsaw puzzle. Sometimes, some change shape or size and pop out like a new flower in a garden from the puzzle. The other colours ensure that the changes are cooperatively reconstructed so that the pieces fit snuggly back into the picture. I have witnessed many such flowers blooming in the beautiful gardens of people. Each has its pathways of beauty lined with trees of feelings, butterflies of thoughts going from moment to moment and fences of emotions tempered by years of experience.

Today, it suddenly started raining, and in this myriad of tales, I was reminded of the beautiful tale in the season of love, 'Sawan'.

It's been two months since Sawan met Baarish on a Sunday afternoon near the shop, which adores the fantastic scenery of the roadside view of the beautiful beach of Gopalpur. Sawan works as a waiter in a famous restaurant in the society, serving mouthwatering dishes. She was 35 years old and was still waiting for her ideal life partner since she was 25.

A partner who would meet her expectations of being loving, understanding, helpful, courteous, polite, handsome, well-mannered, friendly, adorable, and rich.

After being alone for a few years, she realised the twisted expectations she had nurtured in her mind, and her longing for a partner started eroding her expectations one by one. All these perfect qualities she was looking for had created an invisible barrier of silence between her and anyone she met. She was still hopeful of finding her ideal partner when, one day, she saw a handsome man walking on the pathway outside the restaurant. It was love at first sight.

Her heart started beating rapidly, and the thrill of a pleasurable cool breeze suddenly invaded her body. A single drop of sweat formed on her brow and started flowing down. Her mind wanted the man to look at her, and low behold, the man turned towards her, smiled, and moved on his way. This sequence of events started every day with the smile turning to a wave with the palm of the hands and, at times, accompanied by raising the eyebrows. Sawan learned his name was Baarish, and he was as mature as her. However, they had still not spoken to one another. Every day, the man would pass by the window of the restaurant, wave his hand, and instil another ray of hope into Sawan. Sawan also concluded that the name Baarish had been made to be with Sawan always. When she shared her feelings for the man with her roommates, they suggested she declare her love to Baarish. Sawan thought of many ways; she read books on how to propose, watched YouTube videos and saw movies on love. But she could not gather the courage to go ahead with her plan. One day, she had an early morning dream in which she saw herself living with her love in a beautiful house by the side of a serene pond full of lotus flowers in full bloom.

Sawan took the indication as that for her to take the plunge. She got up, put on her best-suited yellow dress, the one she had preserved for the special occasion, did make-up, curled her hair into strands of fluffy bundles and wore the high-heeled sandals that made her appear gorgeous while being vulnerable. That day, she carried her smile to the restaurant and waited with patience for the time of the meeting to arrive.

She was biting her nails and adjusting her dress very frequently.

As the Baarish passed in front of the restaurant came close, she took her spot closer to the door with the bouquet of white roses she had specially purchased for the occasion. She spotted Baarish from a distance. He was wearing a light blue shirt with the top button remaining undone. His dark blue jeans were a perfect match with his shirt. In her excitement, she completely missed the companion that Baarish was with, and before she could speak, Baarish introduced his companion, Megha. The introduction struck Sawan like lightning. She felt as though a current of 1000 volts was passing through her body. She felt dizzy, and her legs were giving away from under her. She held on to the wooden door to prevent herself from falling. Sawan felt as though her dreams were shattered.

Her mind was probing and pondering, 'What made Megha better suited for Baarish than Sawan?' Slowly, she came back to her senses and realised that it was her assumptions that had led to this situation of despair. As the initial wave of sadness passed by, Sawan offered the bouquet to Megha and wished her and Baarish a strong bond with unbreakable companionship growing with the years. She walked away with a sweet smile into the world of hopes and dreams, waiting for her 'Baarish' who, far away, was hearing the rhythmic humming of the song 'Sawan ko Aane do...'

Uma Srikar

An ardent learner by birth, Uma Srikar has explored many fields apart from her academics (Masters in Mathematics, BHU) followed by working in corporate (ex-banker in MNC, Mumbai). Since 2007, she has been diving deep into different alternative healing modalities which led her to get certified in some and gain expertise in some other. A few of them are Gratitude, Forgiveness, Mindfulness, Chakra Meditation, Bach Flower Remedies, Mandala Therapy, Switch words, Pranayama, Music Therapy, Access Consciousness (Bars) and NLP (trainer). A nature lover, Uma Srikar is fine-tuned to create a melody with her 5 favourite notes i.e., Curiosity, Clarity, Creativity, Confidence and Compassion, that aligns her system magically. From this zone, whatever she creates, leaves a lasting impact. To take forward her mission to help people transform through simple yet effective lifestyle changes she has founded Padm-Smriddhi (Lotus of Prosperity). She strongly believes in genuinely nourishing the roots for the tree of life to bloom to its BEST potential.

Tom & Jerry by Uma

"Take this. Take this also. ...a.....um.....please please take this also na...and.."

"Enough!" I blurted.

These little fights between us, the siblings, were as entertaining and rejuvenating as watching the Tom and Jerry series after a long tiring and boring day at work.

Sunday mornings were always special. Waking up smelling the refreshing aromas of filter coffee, chattering of neighbours, who would come just to say hi yet get into long mundane conversations at the top of their voice. The sounds of bells from nearby temples, soothing voice of Anup Jalota from the kitchen radio made a permanent place in my heart. Even now, after 35 years I am transported to childhood with the perfect blend of temple bells and Anup Jalota songs.

The day continued with the heavenly experience of pure human bonds weaved by the threads of mutual trust and respect, common values, and zeal for living life to the fullest.

Rama, my third brother would strategically wait patiently for the moment I get busy with washing my clothes. And I? Knowing that, I would somehow give in to his appeal and end up cleaning his clothes too. I would keep finding reasons to avoid him and delay the process. I would wait for him to step out for his cricket practice. He was good at reading my mind. The moment I enter the washroom, soak my clothes in soap water, he would come back pretending to pick up his cricket kit or water bottle. And then he would turn to me with his wide eyes, big smile, heart jumping with joy as if that was his Eureka moment.

This will follow with the above routine "take this...take this also...." conversation. I would feel defeated in the cold-war that we were into since early morning. Despite this, a part within, would be satiated as we soak ourselves in the adventure of this hide and seek game. This seemingly tricky situation always ended up with a hearty laugh while we reflected upon who fooled whom, to what extent and how.

***

The Music of Bondings

It was 10pm on a winter night in Northern India.

"You go, sleep. I will record this program for you. Listen to it tomorrow after coming back from school."

"Aha! That sounds great !!" I thought.

Nana, my second brother as usual with this sweet gesture once again made me understand "how to nurture a loving bond through genuine concern and action."

Those days the only medium to experience LIVE Classical Music from the comfort of home was Doordarshan. And the tape recorder was the way to record those programs.

I was keen in enhancing my musical skills and I had the support of my parents and siblings. My brothers would take me to various late night classical music concerts.

Despite the delightful offer I was glued to television.

"Just 5 more mins please.", I pleaded without taking my eyes away from the television.

I wanted to remain in the world of trance that the great musicians had skilfully taken me into. The offer was logically perfect yet soulfully unsatiating. Just like Lays Chips. Once you open the packet you can't stop at one. I was wanting more. And then a little more.

He approved and patiently waited for me to leave on my own. My nth request was a decisive one. He gave me a stern look and I knew it's time to pull the rajai over my head and sleep soundly.

Tom and Jerry's story with Nana was unique. Here, he would push me for things that's beneficial for ME yet I would resist due to childish ignorance.

While listening to the recording for almost 4 hrs, the next day, I realized that my second brother, Nana didn't sleep till midnight and got up very early as usual as he had to go to office by 7am.

A night without sleep makes your body feel like a flickering candle, waiting to lie down any moment. Yet somehow, they magically managed to show up with their usual energy and enthusiasm for life, the next day.

That day, the seed of compassion in me was deeply nurtured.

***

The Timeless Symphony

"What happened? Whom are you looking around for? How come you haven't gone to school yet?

"The school rickshawala hasn't come yet. I am getting late." I complained with my raised and fiery eyes and red face. I presented him with a cocktail of emotions of anger, anxiety, worry, helplessness, and sadness with my tonality. It wasn't palatable at all. Still Nana maintained his calm.

He parked his bike next to the main door and stood next to me for a few moments, with his one hand over my shoulder. He was in deep thoughts. This was his office timings too and the inspection was going on. My school and his office were in 2 different directions. My emotions were oscillating between the anger towards rikshawala and worry about what if I get late. Thinking of any solution was far from my reach.

“Let’s go. Sit behind.” Suddenly, he commanded and took out the keys, and started the bike with just one kick.

“Haan?” I was taken aback. Pleasantly though.

“Hurry up! I will drop you and then go to the office.”

He confidently said while looking ahead and raising the accelerator a bit to keep the bike roaring.

“Umm yes, ok...and....” I was perplexed. I didn’t want him to be late either.

He cut me short by gesturing me to sit.

With mixed feelings of happiness, worry, anger...I pushed myself to go with him. Any other solution was out of sight for me.

I handed over my school bag, climbed onto the bike and put my hands over his shoulder and wooooooossssshhhhhh......I arrived at my school in no time.

During my exams he ensured I never get late for my school. He would see that I sleep on time and wake up on time. He would push me to get ready for school before time. In case the rickshawala was not there on time, he himself would accompany me to the school. He helped me throughout my school days in every way with my studies.

When I look back now, I realize that I was their first priority. It makes my heart brim with pride and happiness. I feel highly valued. A big broad smile effortlessly lights up my face. It stays for hours without losing its shine. I pray for their well-being, silently. And feel grateful for such selfless and supporting people who endlessly work to enhance the quality of my life by adding such heart touching human experiences.

There are innumerable such instances that make me feel rich within. Recalling these experiences works as a booster dose. It improves my immunity towards negativity and helps me overcome the challenges of life while I stay away from my siblings now and have moved way forward in life, in a different direction, all by myself, hiding a deep desire within, to cross the pathways once again and laugh and have fun together.

Gratitude to Rama and Nana for always being loving, caring, understanding and compassionate towards my needs and for being magnanimous to ignore my loud voice, constant irritating arguments, silly fights, saying NO due to high ego, and many many other flaws.

I believe it is your childhood experiences that MAKE you or BREAK you.

I am fortunate to have experienced the BESTEST of moments possible. It will remain with me throughout my life.

Pearls of these memories would always adorn the beauty in and around me. And I am so happy about it.

Memories are the BEST gift you can offer to anyone. Isn't it?

www.ingramcontent.com/pod-product-compliance
Lightning Source LLC
LaVergne TN
LVHW021144160826
845679LV00023B/2046

* 9 7 9 8 8 9 2 7 7 0 7 1 2 *